# WHAT TED SAID

A collection of poems, cartoons and stories

by

# JOHN MASON

Published in Great Britain

Copyright © John Mason 2023

John Mason asserts the moral right to be
identified as the author of this work

All rights reserved. No part of this publication may
be reproduced, stored in a retrieval system, or transmitted
in any form or by any means: electronic, mechanical,
photocopying, recording or otherwise, without the prior
permission of the author or his representative.

## CONTENTS

| | |
|---|---|
| About the author | 5 |
| Ode to a Teddy Bear | 7 |
| A dangerous Job | 8 |
| The Pals | 9 |
| Susie | 10 |
| Jake's Poem | 11 |
| Jake's Story | 12 |
| Jake's Monster | 16 |
| Emma | 17 |
| Hoppy the Kangaroo | 18 |
| Letter from Lapland | 20 |
| Winter | 22 |
| The Fielder Family in 2032 | 23 |
| Ted Goes Fishing | 24 |
| The Last Clean | 28 |
| Cannibals | 29 |
| Alone | 39 |
| Ted and the Crocodile | 40 |
| The Little Man | 44 |
| The Interview | 45 |
| Another Day | 46 |
| Poker-Man | 48 |
| Dignity in Dementia | 50 |
| Murphy's Rocket | 51 |
| The Bow Tie Song | 54 |
| Inventions to Catch a Dog | 56 |
| Christmas Comes Early in Ted's House | 61 |
| Sea Levels | 64 |
| My Cousin Sid | 65 |
| Dressing Up Dogs | 66 |
| Forget the Past | 67 |
| The Wighton Parrot | 68 |
| Covid 19 | 75 |
| Lifes Too Short | 75 |
| The Last Pork Pie | 76 |
| Not Just a Dog | 78 |

## ABOUT THE AUTHOR

John Mason was born at Woodford Green, Essex in 1934. The family evacuated to Norfolk during the War to live with his Grandmother in Wighton. He was called up for National Service as a lorry driver, an enjoyable time which will be the subject of a separate book later.

On returning from the Army to Briston, John married Jean and they had a daughter Julie. She married Steven and they had three sons, Jake, Bruce and Freddie. John was an enthusiastic Dad and Grandad, with a wild imagination and great sense of humour. Jean died of dementia in 2015, with John having been her carer for many years.

John had various jobs throughout his life, starting in the building trade and retiring as a driving instructor at the age of 76. He was a doorman at West Runton Pavilion, and his memories of that time were the inspiration behind the book 'What Flo Said.

John was fearless: always ready to take on a challenge, to be the first person on the dance floor, to break an awkward silence with a quip. He loved music, often singing, whistling, or playing the mouth organ, and he enjoyed driving and dancing, although not all at the same time, as he probably would have said.

In later life, John met Helen at a dance in Sheringham and they were together for 5 years. They had many trips away, danced several times a week and enjoyed each other's company.

John had a deep empathy with animals, owning several dogs and looking after several more, one of whom used to email the owners while they were away! John wrote many stories and poems, and often produced illustrations of humorous scenarios he imagined. These were compiled into a booklet in 2007, called 'What Ted Said' after one of his recurring characters. This latest edition was produced posthumously by his daughter and includes John's later works arranged, as far as artistic licence allowed, in chronological order.

For someone who tried to make the most of every day, and live life to the full, it was fitting that John died suddenly whilst out dancing, in December 2023.

He will be sadly missed by all who knew and loved him, but he leaves us with a legacy of fun, humour and many great anecdotes. He will be remembered fondly as a Legend in our time.

## ODE TO A TEDDY BEAR
*Written for his daughter Julie in the late 1960s*

Edward, Edward, so dirty white,
Where will you be sleeping tonight?
My bed is full, oh can't you see
You'll have to sleep down on the settee.

'Please don't make me,' said the poor little Bear,
'It gets so very, very, very cold in here.
Please don't make me sleep on the floor
And I promise you that I won't snore.'

# A DANGEROUS JOB

## THE PALS

Out from the cart shed came a bedraggled, shaggy mess.
'Go away,' the farmer said, 'You're nothing but a pest.
You chase my sheep, you kill my hens, from that you get much fun.
One day it will be fatal, for I'll get you with my gun.'

This day was not too far away for, while in an empty chicken hut,
The wind it blew, the door it swung and 'BANG!' was tightly shut.

For five long days and five long nights freedom never came,
To this little, dirty, scruffy dog, his heart began to pain.
He thought of all the days gone by when freedom was his own,
He fast began to think this was his last, his final home.

The farmer opened up the door and in the shed did peep.
There on the floor, all rough and weak, was Paddy fast asleep.
He closed the door and bolted tight and to the farm did run.
He rushed back even faster, and took aim with his gun.

His finger touched the trigger, the final blow to make,
When a little brown eye opened, then the other, this mess it was awake.

The farmer couldn't do it now, he lowered down his gun.
He'd never seen such friendly eyes as they glittered in the sun.
'Come on, old pal,' the farmer said, 'You'll need a bit to eat.
I'll take you to the farmhouse and find you out some meat.'

They're great pals now and Paddy's got the freedom of the farm.
He ignores the hens, and rounds the sheep so they never come to harm.
He likes the farmer's wife as well, despite that nasty bath,
For now he spends the cold winter nights on the farmer's big, warm hearth.

## SUSIE

I'm just an ordinary dog, you see
Waiting patiently for my tea.

The meat is out, the knife is chopping,
All hell's let loose, the scales are dropping.

I'm in the hall now, it's safe you see
As I'm waiting patiently for my tea.

## JAKE'S POEM

I've been around a long time now,
I'm nearly two you see,
But after all this time has passed
Some things still puzzle me.

Why do I have to have a wash
And clean clothes, my Mummy said,
When all I've done since that last bath
Is spend ten hours in bed?

Another thing that puzzles me,
But I'm not sure I should say,
When I get up in the morning,
My Daddy goes to bed all day.

My Mummy says he works on shifts,
I wonder if that means
He earns the money to feed us all
Working in his dreams.

# JAKE'S STORY
*Written September 1990*

This is the house at Wood Dalling where a little boy called Jake lives with his little brother Bruce and his Mummy and Daddy. He also has two dogs, one called Jess and one called Fudge. There are some fish in a big glass bowl full of water. Outside there are two ferrets and lots of chickens, who spend all day clucking and scrapping with their feet to find food.

One day Jake was looking out of the window at some cows in Farmer Peter's field. There were some black ones and some brown ones. Just then the 'phone rang, BRR BRR … BRR BRR, and his Mummy rushed to answer it.

It was his Daddy, 'phoning from work to ask if Jake and Bruce were all right. Mummy told him Bruce was playing with some toys and Jake was being good counting the cows in Farmer Peter's field. 'One, two, three,' she heard him count.

Jake had counted up to five when his Mummy came back into the room. 'Daddy would like you to tell him how many cows there are in the field,' she said.

'I don't know,' said Jake, 'I haven't finished counting them yet, but I will tell him when he comes home from work.'

Mummy went off to tell Daddy what Jake was going to do, but Jake could not remember how many cows he had counted.

'One, two, three, four,' Jake started counting again, 'Five, six, seven, eight ... .'

Just then Mummy came back into the room again. 'Will you look after Bruce, please,' she said, 'I'm going to cook the dinner.' As Jake always likes to help he was very pleased to do it.

Jake looked out of the window again at the cows, but alas he could not remember how far he had counted. He thought for a moment and then he had an utterly brilliant idea. 'I know what I will do,' he said out loud. 'Each time I count a cow I will press one of my fingers onto the window sill. That way I will always remember how far I have counted.

Jake looked out of the window again and saw Farmer Peter arrive on his tractor with a load of hay to feed to the cows. When Farmer Peter had finished unloading the hay and the cows were standing very still eating it, he counted them to see if any had got out of the field and may be lost.

Jake started counting again, this time using his fingers so he could remember how many he had counted if Mummy came in and spoke to him.

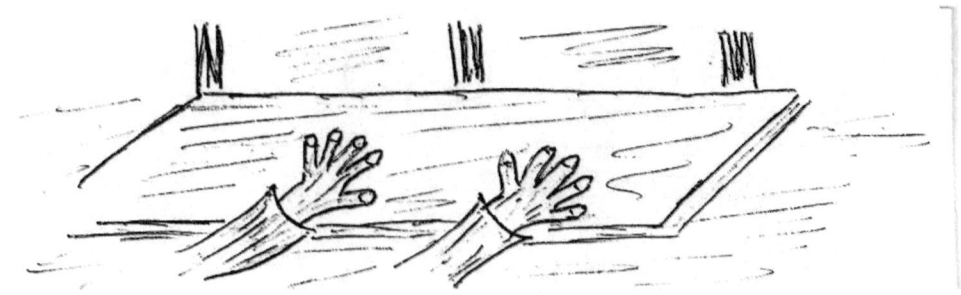

'One,' he pressed his little finger down onto the window sill. 'Two, three, four,' and when he got to five he pressed his thumb down. 'Six,' he pressed down the thumb on his other hand, 'Seven, eight, nine, ten.' He had counted all the cows and had all his fingers pressed down onto the window sill. 'Now this is going to be easy. When Daddy comes home, all I will have to do is count my fingers,' though Jake.

Jake spent the rest of the day helping his Mummy and playing with little brother Bruce and talking to Fudge and Jess. He soon forgot all about Farmer Peter's field and the cows.

It was late and Jake and Bruce had been in the bath and were ready to go to bed when they heard a car come into the drive. 'It's Daddy home,' said Mummy, and a few moments later the door opened and Daddy came in.

'Hello Jake, hello Bruce,' said Daddy, 'Have you all had a busy day?'

Mummy said Bruce had been playing with his toys and Jake had been counting cows in Farmer Peter's field.

'How many cows were in the field?' Daddy asked Jake.

Jake had forgotten how many, but remembered there were the same number of cows as he had fingers. Jake started counting. His little finger was number one, then two, three, four, five was his thumb, six was the thumb on his other hand, seven, eight, nine, ten. 'There are ten cows in the field,' he told his Daddy.

'How did you remember?' Daddy asked.

'I counted on my fingers,' said Jake.

Daddy thought this was very clever and said that one day maybe Jake would teach Bruce to count like that.

As Jake lay in bed that night he could hear the cows mooing and he wondered if, when he woke up in the morning, there would still be ten. 'Maybe I'll count them again tomorrow,' he thought.

'Good night cows,' he said, and he was sure he heard ten cows mooing 'Good night' back to him.

## JAKE'S MONSTER

Jake's monster isn't brown or white,
He's not even slightly that,
You can't see him in the dark, dark night,
As he's totally, totally black.


His orange eyes were bright and round,
As macaroni he did see.
'It's breakfast time, well I'll be bound,
With a nice big cup of tea.'


A stegosaurus he looks like,
As he walks along the trail.
One foot left and one foot right,
And a great big, long black tail.


He's lovely, friendly and nice to see,
Wobbling on his two big feet.
Called 'Staggeringsaurus' he should be,
A staggeringsaurus black and neat.

## EMMA

When Emma to the loo did go
To have a very much needed po,
She looked around to see this treat
And quick as a flash the turd did eat.

Her mistress with the shovel came,
Emma thought this a fabulous game.
'Where's it gone?' her mistress said,
To Emma, now behind the shed.

# HOPPY THE KANGAROO

A little boy called Ted sat watching the television when he heard that a kangaroo called Hoppy had escaped from the local zoo. It had jumped over the fence and ran away. The man on the television said the kangaroo was very friendly and if anyone saw it he would like them to try to catch it.

Ted's Mummy and Daddy said it would be a good idea if they all went out in the car to see if they could find the kangaroo and Ted said he would take the dog's lead to put on it if they found it. His Mummy thought this was a very good idea.

They decided to take their two dogs with them as their noses would soon be able to smell out another animal. They were soon all in the car and Ted's Daddy was about to drive off when Ted realised he would need his binoculars if they were going to stand any chance of finding the escaped kangaroo. His Mummy rushed indoors, collected the binoculars and they were soon on their way.

It was a very hot day, the car windows were open and the two dogs had their heads out, sniffing at the air. Ted's Daddy drove a long way and all the time Ted was looking through his binoculars. Then he suddenly realised he didn't know what a kangaroo looked like.

He thought to himself, 'If it can jump high, it can't be as big as a horse or a cow. Maybe it has got some kind of wings. No,' he decided, 'That would mean it would fly.'

Just then, as he looked through the binoculars, he saw a head above a hedge, then it went down and then came up again. Ted thought this was very strange and asked his Daddy to stop the car. The two dogs in the car were now barking very loudly. They could not see as far as Ted with his binoculars but they could smell that another animal was about. Ted's Daddy said he would take one of the dogs' leads and if it was the kangaroo maybe he could get the lead over its head.

Mummy, Ted and the two dogs waited patiently but they did not have to wait long, for suddenly they heard 'bong, bong, bong, bong,' and round the corner came Daddy leading the kangaroo as it bounced up and down. Ted looked in amazement at this new animal which was like a big dog, but with very long back legs. It used these to spring itself up and down. It was very friendly but very difficult to touch as it never stopped bouncing up and down.

It was not possible to get the kangaroo into the car so they decided that Mummy would lead it first, then Daddy would lead it while Mummy drove the car. Ted was pleased he was the last one to lead it as this meant he could take it through the zoo gates and hand it over to the zoo keeper.

The zoo keeper was very pleased and said Ted could come to the zoo anytime he liked and he would not have to pay any money to get in. Ted was still puzzled by this strange animal and he asked the zoo keeper why it jumped up and down so much.

'I don't know,' replied the zoo keeper, 'but it jumps extra high in the summer but not at all in the winter when the snow is on the ground. Perhaps it is happy in the summer and thinks it is back home in very hot Australia on the other side of the world.' The zoo keeper said he could not make the fence any higher so he would have to send the kangaroo back to Australia.

Ted said goodbye to Hoppy the kangaroo and went sadly back to the car. He didn't speak all the way home, all he could think of was poor old Hoppy going all the way to Australia on the other side of the world.

The rest of the day he spent drawing kangaroos and sometimes hopping up and down, but he found that very tiring and was ready for bed a little earlier than usual. Ted's Daddy decided to fill the bath as Mummy was still washing up. When it was ready he shouted to Ted to come and get into it. Ted placed his foot into the water and immediately lifted it out again. 'This water is much too hot,' he said, 'It burnt my foot and made me jump.' Ted thought and thought and thought. 'I wonder..., I wonder...., I know!' he shouted.

Mummy rushed in from the kitchen screaming, 'Whatever is the matter, Ted?'

'I know,' Ted shouted. 'I know why kangaroos jump up and down. It is very hot in Australia and it is hot here in the summer. When I touched the hot water just now it made me jump because I burnt my foot. I think kangaroos burn their feet on the ground when it's hot and that is why they jump.'

Ted's Daddy put some cold water into the bath and Ted bathed himself and went to bed. He lay thinking, 'If only I could do something to keep Hoppy the kangaroo in the zoo.' He thought and thought and thought and then, 'I know, I know,' he said, 'I will go to the zoo tomorrow and put some shoes onto Hoppy's two big back feet. That will stop them getting hot and then he won't jump so high.'

The next day, Ted rushed to the zoo. Hoppy was being loaded onto a big lorry which was going to take him to Australia on the other side of the world. Ted had brought a big pair of his Daddy's shoes with him and he told the zoo keeper his idea. 'Please let me put these shoes onto Hoppy to see if they will stop him jumping over the zoo fence.' The zoo keeper said he could give it a try and if Hoppy was good he would be able to stay at the zoo.

\*\*\*\*

Hoppy the kangaroo never jumps over the fence with his shoes on and in the winter they are taken off. Ted goes every week to see Hoppy and he often take his friends as well. They have all grown very fond of Hoppy and, although Ted has told the story many times, they still like to hear how Hoppy came to be the kangaroo with shoes on.

*(Illustration by Julie Fielder)*

# LETTER FROM LAPLAND
*From Santa Claus!*

18th December 1996

Dear John

I was pleased to receive your letter but it was a little silly of you to wish me a merry Christmas as I have to work and can't get very merry in charge of my reindeer. You also said it must be nice to only have to work once a year. Can I remind you I have been working in the shops for over two months. I am now quite tired but I will try not to let you down on Christmas Eve.

You said you would like a Jaguar for Christmas and was clearing your garage to put it in. I don't want to sound a grumpy Claus but you cannot keep a jaguar in a garage, it will have to have a proper cage.

I must also point out you won't get it for six months as it must go into quarantine to prevent the spread of infection when it first comes into this country. Anyway, why can't you have a dog like any normal person?

You asked me what it was like living in Lapland. Well, not very nice. I have to look after the reindeer all the year and people like you wait till just before Christmas to write to me, then it's only because you want a present. Then you expect me to deliver on time, and to add to that I have no-one to bring me any presents. I'm also fed up with my red clothes – some people think I'm a post box if I stop in the street.

Well, I must go as I can hear Mrs Claus shouting from the other end of the grotto. I think she wants me to take her to Asda to do some Christmas shopping. One of the reindeer is not very good in the snow so while I am that way I'm going to take it to my brother Clip-Their Claus, who is a vet, to get some snow shoes fitted.

All the best, Santa Claus

## WINTER

Winter's here, its long, dull days,
Distant views blanked off with haze.
Roadmen cover icy roads with grit,
As the farmer goes by with trailer-loads of manure.

The plough the harvest stubble turns,
Seagulls follow, looking for worms.
The ploughman looks, his teeth doth grit,
As the farmer goes by with trailer-loads of manure.

The franchised milkman rushes to the door,
It says 'leave three,' so make it four.
Holes in the milk tops, I'll kill that tit,
As the farmer goes by with trailer-loads of manure.

Christmas gets near, tree lights flash,
Shoppers make their final dash.
Cliff Richard sings his Christmas hit,
As the farmer goes by with trailer-loads of manure.

The farmer's Christmas lunch was fine,
Shared with friends from back some time.
His wife was pleased for one day he'd quit
From going by with trailer-loads of manure.

# THE FIELDER FAMILY IN 2032

# TED GOES FISHING

A heap of bedclothes moved and a sleepy head appeared above the sheets. It was Ted awaking to the first day of his school holiday. 'Ah,' he said, 'Awake again, I seem to do this every morning, what a bore.'

He slid out of bed, staggered to the window and looked out over the meadows and down to the river below. 'It's a nice bright sunny day, I'll go fishing.'

He dashed to the bathroom, quickly washed and dressed and rushed down the stairs to the kitchen.

'Hello Ted,' said his mum. 'You have just missed your dad, he said he had to leave early today as he had a lot on. He looked as if he had the same clothes on as usual to me.'

'I'm going fishing,' said Ted, 'They should be biting well today.'

'You had better put some good thick gloves on then,' said his mum, 'If they bite you, you never know what you might catch, maybe rabies or the like.'

'I'll have a cup of tea before I leave,' said Ted, and went to plug in the kettle, but it was missing.

'You have done it again,' he said to his mum and went to the kitchen door, opened it and picked up the kettle form the doorstep. 'Dad should never have bought you a kettle the same colour as the cat,' he said, 'I suppose it's been out there all night.'

'No,' said his Mum, 'I saw it sitting on the mat washing a few minutes ago.'

Ted drank his tea, said goodbye to his mum and rushed out of the house and down to the river. He then rushed back to the house to get his fishing rod. He had been fishing about an hour when he heard a big splash. He looked up river and saw a policeman struggling with a man in the water. The man threw a box at the policeman which hit him in the face. The man then ran off with the policeman in hot pursuit. Ted watched as the box floated down the river towards him. As it got near he cast his line and hooked the handle and pulled the box to the bank.

'Gosh,' exclaimed Ted, 'It's a jewel box.' He picked it up and rushed to the police station and handed it to the duty sergeant. Ted then rushed home to tell his mum of his exciting find.

'Hello Ted,' said his mum. 'I'm just preparing the Sunday lunch.' This puzzled Ted as it was only Wednesday.

His mum said she had spent most of the morning looking for the recipe book which she always read to Ted before he went to bed. Ted could not understand why she needed it as she was only doing boiled eggs and buttered soldiers.

'I think there is a knock at the door,' said his mum. Ted rushed to see what a knock looked like. He opened the door and saw to his surprise a policeman with a plaster on his nose.

'I wonder why they call policemen "knocks",' he thought.

'DAR DOO DED?' the policeman asked.

Ted was taken aback by this. Into the kitchen, in fact, as he had caught his braces on the kitchen taps. As Ted was climbing out of the sink he said to his mum, 'There's a policeman at the door and he wants to know if I'm dead.'

'You can't be dead,' said his mum, 'I'm still drawing Family Allowance for you. Unhook your braces from the taps and let's see what he wants.'

She led the way out of the kitchen and tripped over a sausage roll she used as a door stop. Her head went into the goldfish bowl and she slid through the hall under a big mat halfway along and came to a stop at the front door.

The startled policeman looked down. 'DEEP DOUR DOD DUNDER DONDOLE DOUNG DAN,' he said to Ted. Ted's mum clambered to her feet complete with goldfish bowl on her head and a goldfish sticking out of each ear.

'MIME MED'S MUM, MOW MAM MI MELP MOU,?' said Ted's mum.

The policeman with plaster on his nose then went on to say how Ted was wanted at the police station in connection with the finding of the stolen jewels. The three of them walked to the police car, Ted got into the front with the driver and his mum got into the back with the policeman with the plaster on his nose.

'I am going via the hospital so my colleague can get his nose fixed, then I will take you and your mum on to the police station,' the driver said and, with blue lights flashing, they set off.

At the police station Ted's mum had a problem convincing the station duty sergeant she was not from another planet, but he eventually arranged for the fire brigade to come and remove the goldfish bowl.

'I'm Sergeant Watch-What-You-Are-Doing Brown, and before you ask, I got the name because when I was being Christened the vicar dropped me into the font just as he asked "What name giveth this child?" and my father shouted out, "Watch what you are doing!"'

He sat behind his big desk, looked at Ted and his mum and went on to say how his name had held him back all his life and he was sure he would have had a much higher rank in the police force if he hadn't had a name like Brown.

'My mother always felt sorry for me,' he said, 'and, so I didn't feel inferior about my Christian names, she called my younger brother Mary Alice, she said it was suggested by her Uncle Elsie. Well,' the Sergeant continued, 'That's enough of my problems. You are the hero of the day, Ted, and I have been asked to take you to the Squire's big house on the hill to collect your reward for finding and returning the stolen jewels.'

The Sergeant jumped to his feet and quickly sat down again. He had forgotten he had lent his trousers to the other policeman after he had fallen into the water.

'I'll phone the big house and ask them to send the chauffeur with the Rolls Royce to pick you up.'

Ted was thrilled with the thought of this, he had never been in a Rolls Royce before. His mum was already sitting on a chair practicing her wave and saying things like, 'What a splendid little car,' and, 'I must get one of these to go to the shops in.'

A few minutes later a car stopped outside, the door of the police station opened and in walked a tall man wearing a peaked cap. He suddenly realised he was only wearing a peaked cap and rushed out again.

Ted and his mum decided to walk to the big house on the hill. They set off through the main street and turned into the road that wound its way up to the Squire's mansion. As they walked up the hill they passed big heaps of settees, tables, tea trolleys, and even beds with the sheets still on them. Just then they heard a rumbling noise and around the corner came an armchair with a little man sitting in it. He waved, whizzed past and crashed into the big heap of furniture. Ted and his mum looked in amazement as the little man picked up the newspaper he was reading and started walking up the hill towards them.

'I'm getting really fed up with this,' he said. 'It's all the fault of my great grandfather who built the house halfway up the hill. Not knowing much about building he made it slope the same as the hill and if we forget and open the wrong door the furniture runs out. I'm the Squire, by the way.'

'I've never met a Squire before,' said Ted, 'You must be very rich.'

'Yes, I am very rich,' replied the Squire. 'My family made their fortunes abroad growing square bananas, saved a fortune on shipping costs as they fitted into the cardboard boxes better than the ones you get today.'

The Squire went on to say how he was to carry on the family tradition of making lots of money. He had invented a one-wheeled tractor with a wheel no wider than a bicycle wheel. 'It will run over the fields without damage to the crops.'

'What stops a one-wheeled tractor falling over?' asked Ted.

'Ah,' said the Squire, 'That's the only problem I have yet to solve.'

The Squire invited Ted and his mum up to the big house for afternoon tea. As they approached the huge iron gates the Squire told how the house had been burgled and a box of jewels stolen. 'That reminds me,' he said, 'I can't entertain you long as I have a young man by the name of Ted coming to collect his reward.'

'I'm Ted,' said Ted.

'Fancy that,' said the Squire, 'Two people by the name of Ted coming to my house in one day.'

As the Squire and his visitors approached the front door, four huge lions pulled on chains and stopped just short of them.

'How did anyone steal jewels from a house guarded by lions?' exclaimed Ted.

'The problem was,' said the Squire, 'I could not get anyone to untie them when the robbers were about.'

They entered the house and went into a huge drawing room with its slanting ceiling, walls and floor. The Squire then repeated that they could not stay long as he had this young man called Ted coming up from the police station to collect his reward. Ted's mum put her cup down onto the small table and they all watched as it slipped to the floor, out through the open French doors, across the lawn and out of sight down the hill.

'Sir,' she said, 'This is the Ted you are waiting for, he is the one you are giving the reward to.'

'Delighted to meet you, what a great pleasure this is,' and with that the Squire reached out to shake Ted by the hand. 'Well done, well done.'

He rang the service bell and asked the butler to bring Ted's reward. He then presented Ted with a scroll made of parchment, which said Ted could fish in the Squire's new lake at any time, free of charge.

The Squire then led the way outside. 'Come with me,' he said, 'Come and see the biggest private lake in the world.'

'But you have dug it on the side of a hill,' said Ted.

'Yes,' said the Squire, 'That has caused a few problems but when I can keep the water in it will be the biggest private lake in the world.'

Ted and his mum said goodbye, thanked the Squire for the tea and headed off down the hill for home. As they passed the police station they could hear the policemen having an argument about a pair of trousers which had shrank after getting wet.

When they arrived, Ted's dad was home from work, sitting in the kitchen looking very sad, with a big plaster on his nose.

'What happened to you?' asked Ted's mum.

'DOMEONE DAD DICKED DAT.... .'

Ted could take no more of this in one day and decided to go up to his room. As he climbed the stairs he could hear his dad saying how he came in the front door, tripped over the hall mat someone had left in a heap, slid along the hall and crashed into the kitchen door, which had closed because someone had removed the sausage roll which kept it open.

'I wonder who could have done that?' asked Ted's mum. 'How is your nose?'

'DERY DORE,' said Ted's dad.

Ted looked out of his bedroom window at the river below. 'Maybe tomorrow I'll play football or cricket, or even stay in and watch television. I don't think I will ever dare go fishing again. What a day!'

## THE LAST CLEAN
*Ode to a cleaner on retirement*

When I think of you it's like a dream
A silhouette above a stream.
The water trickles then a sudden gush
That gentle sound of the toilet flush.

You emerge so fresh with your morning glow
Announcing, as if the world should know,
'This is the last winter I'll work for him
I'm not biking down there again, sod 'em.'

You reiterate your winter hate
Of soaking clothes and low wage rate,
But worst of all, the bitter pill
Is walking back up that bloody hill.

And so it arrives, that final day
You fold the duster, put the hoover away.
You get your last pay and shed a small tear
'Now what the hell will I do for the rest of the year?'

# CANNIBALS
*Illustrations for the Mark Knopfler Song,
which John and his grandsons used to sing along to*

# CANNIBALS
*Illustrations for the Mark Knopfler Song,
which John and his grandsons used to sing along to*

# CANNIBALS
*Illustrations for the Mark Knopfler Song,
which John and his grandsons used to sing along to*

# CANNIBALS
*Illustrations for the Mark Knopfler Song,
which John and his grandsons used to sing along to*

# CANNIBALS
*Illustrations for the Mark Knopfler Song,
which John and his grandsons used to sing along to*

## CANNIBALS
*Illustrations for the Mark Knopfler Song,
which John and his grandsons used to sing along to*

# CANNIBALS
*Illustrations for the Mark Knopfler Song,
which John and his grandsons used to sing along to*

## CANNIBALS
*Illustrations for the Mark Knopfler Song,
which John and his grandsons used to sing along to*

# CANNIBALS
*Illustrations for the Mark Knopfler Song,
which John and his grandsons used to sing along to*

## CANNIBALS
*Illustrations for the Mark Knopfler Song,
which John and his grandsons used to sing along to*

## ALONE

The moon filters through the frosted glass
A pattern on the floor.
The clock ticks on, helps time to pass
Its small hand heads to four.


The world's asleep, I'm here alone,
A cold and silent night.
No sound of things like cars or phone,
But something's not quite right.


A muddled night, but fresh in my mind,
An evening just gone by.
Better Indian food would be hard to find,
But I will never even try.


I sit and wonder what went wrong,
I know what not to do,
I've been sitting here for much too long,
When the hell will I get off this loo?

# TED AND THE CROCODILE

Ted got up, looked out of the bedroom window and thought, 'What a lovely day. You don't get many sunny days like this, especially when it's cloudy or raining.' Ted was good at stating the obvious and today was no exception.

Ted thought it would be nice to walk alongside the river to school and maybe throw in a stone or two to see if any fish moved.

Ted washed and went down to breakfast. His Mum was singing to the budgie. She said, 'You know, Ted, I don't think this bird will ever sing. Perhaps as he's from a foreign land he doesn't understand the words.'

Ted ate his breakfast and said he would be leaving a bit early as he was going to school by the river.

'You ought to stick to the road,' said his mum, 'Your feet will be wet all day.'

Ted said his goodbyes and as he went down the garden path he could hear his mum singing *Danny Boy* to the budgie.

Ted walked towards the river, kicking the odd stone as he went and thinking, 'If they call a man who lays bricks a bricklayer, why don't they call a chicken an egglayer?' Ted was a very deep thinker.

He arrived at the river and started to walk alongside it towards school. He threw a stone into the water and as the ripples got wider they glittered in the sunlight but he could not see any fish. Just up river from the bridge was a small island covered in bushes and surrounded by reeds. Ted looked over at the island and thought, 'One day, I will get a boat and row across to explore it. Who knows what I might find, maybe I will be the first person ever to set foot on it. I could claim it as my very own island.'

He threw another big stone into the water. Suddenly, he could hardly believe his eyes. As he looked towards the island he could see rows of huge white teeth glittering in the sunlight. He climbed a nearby tree to get a better view and thought, 'Yes, I think it is, I'm sure it is. Yes, it's a crocodile. A real crocodile.' He could see the teeth disappear as it closed its mouth then reappear as it opened it again. Ted was getting very excited now, but as this was his very own island he would have to be careful who he told about this fantastic discovery.

Ted made his way to school and wondered how he would concentrate on his lessons. He arrived just as everyone was going into assembly, so he would have to wait until mid-morning break before he could tell his best friend Sid about his exciting discovery.

The geography lesson seemed to go on forever. Ted's mind was not on school at all, his only thoughts were his island in the middle of the river. Suddenly he heard a voice shout his name.

'Ted, what is the capital city of France?'

Ted's answer came in a flash. 'Crocodile, Sir,' he said. The teacher looked at him in amazement and all the children in the class started to laugh. Ted felt very embarrassed when the teacher repeated the question, especially as he didn't even know the real answer.

When mid-morning break came, Ted met with Sid to tell him the great news. Sid was sworn to secrecy as Ted made it clear that if news got out about a crocodile in the river there could be panic and maybe someone might come and shoot it.

The friends arranged to meet after school and when the last bell went they raced towards the river. 'If we hurry,' said Ted, 'We'll get there before it gets too dull to see it.' The excitement grew as they approached the river and Ted pointed across towards the island.

'Where is it?' asked Sid. 'I can see the island quite clearly, but no crocodile.'

'You need to get up that tree,' said Ted, pointing, but even then Sid still claimed he could not see it.

'Maybe it's swam off, or perhaps it's sleeping very low in the water,' said Ted. The boys made their way home along the footpath by the river and agreed to discuss the crocodile again the next day.

Ted's dad was home early and was very interested in Ted's discovery. He agreed with Ted it was a very unusual animal to find in the local river. Ted's mum suggested that someone might have brought it from holiday with them and it had escaped.

Ted's dad decided to telephone the local zoo, as the whole family were friends of the manager, but Mr L E Fant could not shed any light on the mystery creature, certainly nothing was missing from the zoo.

Ted watched the News on television that night but there was no mention of an escaped crocodile.

Ted's first thought the next morning was to get down to the river as soon as possible. He was now convinced that no-one believed what he had seen.

It was another lovely sunny morning and Ted hurried along to the spot where he could see the island. He couldn't resist throwing in a few stones to startle the fish and watched the ripples got bigger and bigger as they went towards his island. He climbed the tree and it was there again! The crocodile's mouth was opening and closing, showing its huge white teeth. Ted could not contain himself as he rushed off to school. Assembly had just started. He burst open the door and shouted out, 'Sid, I've seen you-know-what again! It's real, I tell you!'

The headmaster was furious and ordered Ted to wait outside his study so that he could deal with him after assembly.

Assembly seemed to go on forever as Ted waited by the headmaster's door. But Ted wasn't over-concerned as he was preoccupied by what he had seen and by whether he should let the headmaster into his and Sid's secret.

The headmaster strode along the corridor, looking very angry, and ordered Ted into his study.

'Now, Ted,' the headmaster said in a very stern voice, 'I will not have that sort of behaviour. I run a good, tight ship. Tell me, what have you got to say? Speak up, boy.'

Ted's eyes lit up. 'I take it you mean you've got a good tight boat, Sir,' said Ted, 'Not a ship.'

'Make sense, boy,' said the headmaster in an even louder voice.

'Well,' said Ted, 'I suppose I will have to let you into the secret, Sir, that's if you really have got a good, watertight boat. You see, Sir, I've got this island and it's got a crocodile living near it and if we could use your boat we could row over and get a closer look at it. We may even be able to put a rope around it and take it to the zoo. Or, if it's friendly, I might be able to keep it as a pet.'

The headmaster was not at all taken in by what Ted was saying, but he agreed they could ask Mr Shrimp, the fisherman, to bring his rowing boat up river and some of the children could at least go over and explore Ted's island.

The rest of the school day passed in a whirl and when Ted went to bed that night he could hardly sleep for the excitement. Next morning, he took the shortest route to school and arrived early. Mr Shrimp was already waiting and was talking to the headmaster. 'My boat is waiting down on the river,' he was saying, 'And it can carry eight passengers.'

The headmaster told Ted to go and pick another six children to go with them, adding, with a laugh, 'Make sure they are not afraid of crocodiles!'

Ted and his friend Sid decided to only take people who they thought would not get seasick or be afraid of coming face to face with a crocodile, and in no time at all they had rounded up five of their bravest friends.

Mr Shrimp gave everyone a bright orange lifejacket and they all set off with Mr Shrimp rowing very quickly to get the boat started. Ted noticed that even the headmaster was getting excited and, as the boat rounded a bend, everyone looked in amazement at Ted's island, shining in the bright morning sun.

Mr Shrimp was digging the oars into the water and pulling back with great might, causing huge waves to go out from the boat. Ted was beginning to get quite anxious. 'Now what if the crocodile has swam away,' he thought, 'Everyone will think I was making it up.'

Ted peered past Mr Shrimp and there, in the distance, he could see the crocodile, opening its huge jaws wider than ever as the boat got closer to the island.

'Look, there it is!' shouted Ted, and everyone rushed to the side of the boat nearest the island. From his new position in the bottom of the boat, face down on a load of fishing nets, the headmaster urged everyone, in a rather muffled voice, to keep sitting down where they had been in case the boat turned over.

'Well, that net seems to be fine, Mr Shrimp,' the headmaster confirmed, after his unexpected examination of it. But no-one took any notice of him. Their eyes were fixed on the crocodile teeth shining in the bright morning sun. Ted told everyone not to get too excited as the noise might frighten the crocodile away and he suggested that Mr Shrimp should row the boat further down the island as it might be dangerous to land too near the crocodile.

A few minutes later they were all safely off the boat and on to Ted's island. It seemed a very quiet place but, looking through the trees, Ted could see an old wooden hut. He thought for a moment that someone lived on his island but as the hut roof had fallen in he decided it was probably not used any more. This meant that Ted was not the first person to discover the island but this didn't bother him as it was his now.

Mr Shrimp stayed with the boat and Ted led the way along the edge of the island towards where the crocodile had been. He was followed by Sid, then the other children, then the headmaster, who stayed at the back to make sure no-one got lost, and to give him a chance to pick off the odd pieces of fish which seemed to have somehow become attached to his clothing.

As they got closer, Ted could hear a strange 'bong-ping' noise. Ted realised he didn't know what noise a crocodile made, but he didn't say anything to the others. Suddenly the headmaster shouted from the back, 'Wait there, it will be better if Ted and I go and look first, to make sure it's safe.' The headmaster crept through the bushes, followed closely by Ted, who could hardly contain his excitement.

At last they arrived. As Ted came out of the bushes, the headmaster sat down on a fallen tree, his eyes fixed towards the water. Ted's heart sank as he looked past the headmaster and there, partly submerged in the water, was the remains of an old grand piano, the lid over the white keys lifting up and down as the waves in the water hit it.

'Well, Ted,' chuckled the headmaster, 'That's another one of your mysteries solved, but what do we do now?'

'Well,' said Ted, staring at a suspicious lump on the headmaster's jumper, 'If you don't say anything about my mistake over the crocodile, I won't tell the others where that horrible fishy smell is coming from.'

The headmaster agreed. When he and Ted got back through the trees to Sid and the other waiting children, the headmaster, standing carefully downwind of them, told them it was not quite a crocodile in the water but, in his opinion, it would not be safe for them to go any further. He told them it would be much better if they all went back to school and got on with their lessons.

Somewhat saddened and very quiet, the children got back into the boat. As Mr Shrimp rowed away, with the headmaster clinging tightly to his seat this time, the children all peered to have a last glimpse of the crocodile thing and wondered whether Ted would ever let them into the secret.

Ted hasn't been on to the island any more, but he still looks over sometimes and, as he throws stones in the water and watches the ripples getting bigger and bigger, he remembers how close he once was to having a crocodile for a pet.

## THE LITTLE MAN

I wandered through a deserted street,
All alone, no-one to meet,
When tapping from a manhole came,
And a faint-hearted cry, it seemed in pain.

'Hi you in there, what's the problem mate?'
I shouted down a nearby grate.
'Get me out of here is all I say,'
Then I heard him gently float away.

I rushed to the manhole next in line
And lifted the cover just in time.
'Come on, old boy, give me your hand,
I'll help you from this awful land.'

Out came a man not three feet high,
In pin-striped suit, bowler hat and tie.
'I cannot move it,' came a shout of fear,
With frantic tugs at a thing in his ear.

We hailed, and a taxi soon did stop.
The driver looked, his eyes did pop.
'What's that thing stuck in his ear?
My taxi's clean, he's not getting in here.'

The little man just turned to say,
'It's done the world over, every day.
I just flushed the loo while over bent,
I leaned too far and in I went.'

A burly bank robber on the run,
Thinking the little man had a gun,
Threw the bank notes at his feet,
Yelling, 'Don't shoot!' made a fast retreat.

Police sirens wailed from all around
And the little man they did surround.
From a distance a policeman was heard to shout,
'Drop that gun or we'll blast you out!'

With the sewer object in his ear,
The little man just didn't hear.
The object pointed as he turned his head
And the policeman fired and shot him dead.

At the Coroner's Court the very next day
The man in charge was heard to say
'You, the police, just shot in fear?
Self-defence? I pooh-pooh the idea.'

The little man's now buried, with his head
In the direction of the sewer bed.
A plaque is fixed high on the wall,
It reads, 'In memory of a man not three feet tall.'

# THE INTERVIEW
*In tribute to Ribs, a dog who was afraid of thunder*

When we stated you must provide basic equipment Mrs Fielder we do expect more than fir cones, seaweed and a dog that shakes just before a thunderstorm

# ANOTHER DAY

The old man sat near the open fire,
He thought of his past with no future desire.
Through the window a light breeze caused the trees to sway.
'I expect this will be another uneventful day.'

Just then a sound new to his ears
Came from the direction of the stairs.
The old man rushed to investigate
The scene he saw was too much to take.

Water from the attic in torrents came,
The old man rushed to the water main.
The stop-tap jammed, stuck up with rust,
Three sharp hits and the tap was bust.

He sent for a plumber who arrived in haste,
With pipe, hacksaw and jointing paste.
He fixed the leak and to the old man said,
'Tonight you can sleep safely in your bed.'

Sadly for him this was not to be,
When the flood had gone the old man could see
The foundations cracked and open wide.
With a rumble the house began to slide.

The old man quickly reached for his pen
To inform his friends he was now number ten.
He liked his new neighbours the left and the right
But they were still shocked by the unusual sight.

The builders came to underpin,
Their drills and hammers made a terrible din.
Soon the floors were fixed and the carpets laid,
They brushed up the mess, final touches were made.

'It's lunch time now,' the old man said,
'I know, I'll fry some bacon and egg.'
The frying seemed slow, so he turned it on higher
And with a 'whoosh' the pan was on fire.

The flames soon spread around the place,
For the fire brigade the old man did race.
The old man said, 'This is my lucky day,
The fire brigade arrived without delay.'

The decorator to the house did rush,
With paint, paper and pasting brush.
The job soon done, it's nearly three.
'Before you go, it's time for tea.'

The old man thought, 'It's not been dull,
I think I'm getting used to the chaotic lull.'
In the quiet he could hear his neighbour say,
'I can't get out with that house in the way.'

The old man thought he would look around,
Went upstairs and fell to the ground.
'It's my lucky day, I missed my head,
All I've done is broken my leg.'

The ambulance arrived extremely fast,
They put his leg in a plaster cast.
'Use these crutches, you will come to no harm.'
The old man fell over and broke his arm.

The carpenter came to fix the floor,
Accidentally nailed the crutch to the door,
He slammed the door to do the repairs,
Which sent the old man headfirst down the stairs.

'I was lucky,' he said, as he rubbed his sore thighs,
'Just three broken ribs and two big black eyes.
A cup of drink and off to bed.
It's time to go and rest my head.'

The old man knelt and was heard to pray,
'Thank you God for a different day.
Some might think it could not be worse,
But I could have gone off in a big black hearse.'

Just then a Jumbo with its landing wheels down
Knocked his roof all over the town.
The pilot said in shocked dismay,
'I'm sure that house wasn't there yesterday.'

The roofers worked all through the night,
To make it wind and water tight.
As dawn broke they drove away.
It was now the start of another day.

The cuckoo clock down in the hall
Sneezed eight times and fell off the wall.
The old man said, 'It was probably old,
Or maybe died naturally due to the cold.'

The old man sat near the open fire,
He thought of his past with no future desire.
Through the window a light breeze caused the trees to sway.
'I expect this will be another uneventful day.'

Just then a sound came to his ears,
Again from the direction of the stairs
Water from the attic shed...
The rest of this poem you have already read!

# POKER-MAN

Poker-Man lived in a big mansion with his two friends, Nine-Iron and Nine-Iron's brother Flat-Iron. The mansion was owned by Mr Nose and his wife, Heaven. They had three boys Running, Dirty and Blowyour, and a little girl called Button. Their uncle Euthanasia also lived with them, as he had no close family left. He seemed to be happy at his new job in the retirement home nearby.

Mr Nose was Lord Nose until one night he forgot to lock his title away in the safe and someone broke in and stole it. The police have stopped looking for it now, they think it has been smuggled out of the country.

Poker-Man was in the kitchen with Flat-Iron. 'I'm fed up,' said Poker-Man, 'I spend my whole life looking at that old boiler.'

'Shut up,' said Flat-Iron, 'You must not talk about the lady of the house like that.'

'Well,' said Poker-Man, 'Your brother, Nine-Iron, is cleaned every day. He goes in the chauffeur-driven Rolls Royce to the golf course every day, and all we do is sit in this mouldy old kitchen. My end's wearing away, I'm getting shorter by the day, I feel like going to the scrap yard in the sky.'

Flat-Iron was very concerned about Poker-Man. 'What you really need is some iron tablets from the doctors, but as that's not possible I will have a word with my brother Nine-Iron to see if we can get a day out.'

That night, Poker-Man and Flat-Iron made their way along the back hallway. 'I admire you,' said Poker-Man, 'You never seem to get de-pressed, though I suppose irons don't.'

'Stop talking,' said Flat-Iron, 'We must press on.' Poker-Man bounced along and Flat-Iron slid along behind, having the odd grumble about the rough pamment floors. They arrived at the huge door to the cupboard where Nine-Iron was kept.

Poker-Man levered open the door and in they went. This was a whole new world. Never had they seen anything like it: brand new tennis racquets, cricket bats shining with linseed oil, rowing machines, everything clean and bright. They turned and saw the bag with wheels which Nine-Iron lived in.

'I wonder if he's in there,' said Flat-Iron. Then, without warning, Poker-Man stabbed away at the bag with great force. In a flash all the golf clubs jumped out of the bag.

'Hello lads,' said Nine-Iron, 'You're looking good,' and he gave Flat-Iron a friendly hit across his handle. He then turned to Poker-Man. 'Gosh,' he said, 'You look rough, old and worn, you need cheering up.'

'That's why we are here,' said Flat-Iron. 'Poker-Man needs a day out. Can you fix it?'

'Jump in the bag,' said Nine-Iron, 'Get some sleep and look forward to a day out tomorrow.'

Next day they drove to the golf club. Mr Nose was playing his brother Hairy. Towards the end of a very hard game, Mr Nose was ready to hit the winning putt. He pulled Poker-Man from the bag and was about to hit the golf ball. Poker-Man had his eyes shut waiting for the bang, when a mole hill appeared between the ball and the hole. Flat-Iron jumped from the bag, jumped up and down and flattened it in seconds. Mr Nose then, using Poker-Man, took the final winning shot.

Poker-Man and Flat-Iron now go in the Rolls Royce every day. 'You know,' said Poker-Man, 'I feel now I have reached the top, I feel really posh, I think I may start calling myself PoKeMoN!'

# DIGNITY IN DEMENTIA

*Written as part of a project at
Woodstock Nursing Home, Gressenhall*

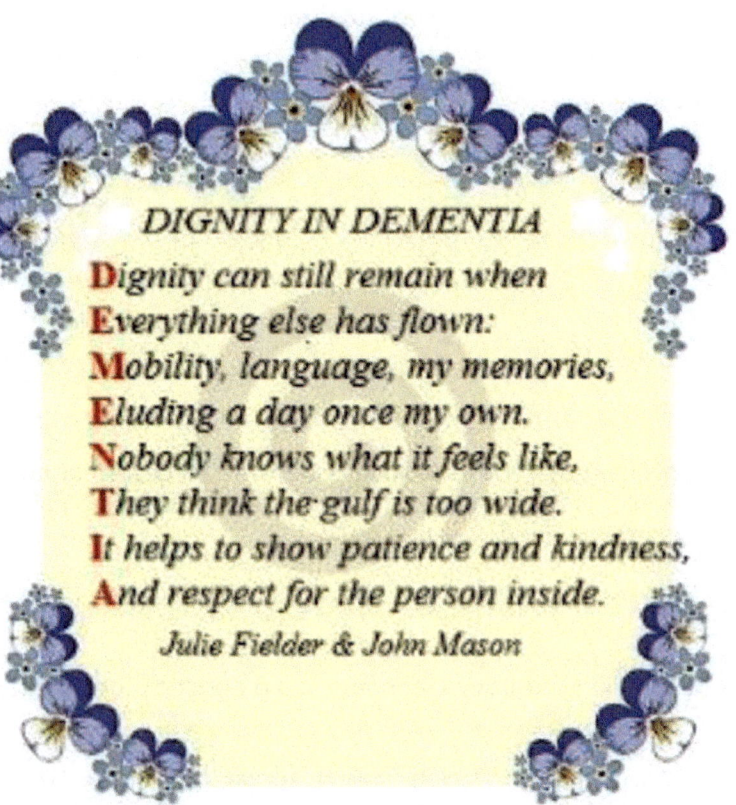

### DIGNITY IN DEMENTIA

Dignity can still remain when
Everything else has flown:
Mobility, language, my memories,
Eluding a day once my own.
Nobody knows what it feels like,
They think the gulf is too wide.
It helps to show patience and kindness,
And respect for the person inside.

Julie Fielder & John Mason

## MURPHY'S ROCKET

Friends Sean, Pat and Murphy
Were never very bright.
Guinness flowed, smoke filled the room,
And singing filled the night.

A silence came across the bar,
Murphy stood to his five feet seven,
'I want you all to be the first to know
I'm building a rocket, to take me to heaven.'

Sitting in the corner
Flannigan donned his cap.
'Sure Murphy, I tink it's a good idea
It'll sure put uz on der map.'

Murphy now had got the crowd,
They looked at him in awe.
He talked of tin and rocket fuel,
Committed, as never before.

In his tin shed on the allotment
Murphy strived to get it right.
Sawing wood and bending tin,
He worked into the night.

Murphy put up posters,
'Diz is what I want to say,
Da rocket launch is tomorrow
But if finished early, it will be yesterday.'

At first light a crowd had gathered,
Today would be the proof.
From the shed stepped hero Murphy
And quickly removed the roof.

A silence came across the crowd,
They could not believe their eyes.
The silver point of shining tin
Reaching to the sky.

Murphy climbed astride the craft
In cycle helmet, goggles and gloves.
He couldn't resist just one more speech
Before entering the clouds above.

'I will return, my friends, from Heaven,
And tell you what I've seen,
So when your day comes to depart this world
You'd tink you've already been.'

The crowd in anticipation stood,
Not a single person spoke.
With the throttle open, then came silence
And a massive cloud of smoke.

A muffled gasp came from the crowd,
The flight was not to be,
A voice was heard within the smoke,
'I tink it needs more dan der fifty cc.'

The weeks rolled on, anticipation grew
As they waited for the news
That Murphy had found an engine
And fixed the final screws.

At the bar just another evening
Of smoking, talk and beer,
When all the room went deadly quiet
An exited voice they could hear.

Murphy burst into the bar
The engine solved it seems,
'Big Bertha Brown will sit in der back
An I'll fire her up wit baked beans.'

At last it was the blast off day,
Again Flannigan donned his cap.
Murphy astride with clipboard and flask
And a full scale AA map.

Murphy thought, 'I'll head it east
And fly right over Devon.
H comes well on after D
Dat should take me on to Heaven.'

He flew on up to London,
And he looked down with delight.
'O sure dis must be Heaven,
O what a Heavenly sight.'

He flew up to the palace,
Stopping with sparks and scrapes.
His eyes looked up in wonderment,
'Jaysus, dees must be the Heavenly gates.'

A man in cap with yellow band
Gave Murphy a steely glare.
'You must have seen the yellow lines,
You can't park that thing here.'

Marlborough to the Strand he went,
And everywhere in between.
He couldn't wait to get back home
To tell them what he'd seen.

Back home the bar was full again
Murphy, the topic as before,
When suddenly the whole bar shook
And Murphy landed with a roar.

The crowd rushed out to greet him back
With a spontaneous three cheers.
Murphy standing aloft the craft, said,
'I have tings to say, pin back yer ears.

Heaven has people from all over der world,
From India, Spain and Thailand,
But I must say I'm a bit concerned
I didn't see any from Ireland.

Soho was a lovely place,
The girls were very nice.
They said they could show me Heaven
But I didn't like the price.

I'm tinking, don't rush to get to Heaven,
Stay here and have a ball.
Keep singing, drinking, enjoy yourself,
While waiting for the call.'

# THE BOW TIE SONG

My father was a dapper man, he carried himself with pride,
I always liked to be with him and stand there by his side.
He had an air about him few people would deny
In pin-stripe suit and brown brogue shoes and a Big Red Dickey-Bow Tie.

One day he called me to his side, his face all gaunt and sad,
'Son, I ask of you the promise I made to my old dad,
My days are up, and I must go to that place up in the sky
Please wear with pride and never remove my Big Red Dickey-Bow Tie.

Now, I know times have changed my son and I understand your plight,
A Big Red Dickey-Bow tie today is not a common sight
But do me this dying favour and to spare you any hurt
Wear the Dickey with great pride my son and cover it with your shirt.'

*'Keep your Dickey under your shirt my boy,' my father said to me,*
*'Keep it tightly covered, so no one else can see*
*The treasure you have hidden there, could fill your life with glee*
*Keep your Dickey under your shirt my boy,' my father said to me.*

Now after Father passed away I wore it there and then,
A promise made by one so young, for I was only ten.
School friends they jeered and laughed at me with a shirt on in PE,
But I never forgot those dying words my father said to me.

*'Keep your Dickey under your shirt my boy,' my father said to me,
'Keep it tightly covered, so no one else can see
The treasure you have hidden there, could fill your life with glee
Keep your Dickey under your shirt my boy,' my father said to me.*

As a strong young man I soon became a lifeguard on the beach,
I saved young girls from drowning if they came within my reach.
My shirt would tend to drag me down as I pulled them from the sea,
But I never forgot those dying words my father said to me

*'Keep your Dickey under your shirt my boy,' my father said to me,
'Keep it tightly covered, so no one else can see
The treasure you have hidden there, could fill your life with glee
Keep your Dickey under your shirt my boy,' my father said to me.*

A pretty young lady said to me after given the kiss of life,
'Wow what did I feel under your shirt, would you take me for your wife?'
I said, 'My love, I'll marry you but some things you'll never see,'
For I never forgot those dying words my father said to me.

*'Keep your Dickey under your shirt my boy,' my father said to me,
'Keep it tightly covered, so no one else can see
The treasure you have hidden there, could fill your life with glee
Keep your Dickey under your shirt my boy,' my father said to me.*

For two long years we courted, the love could not compare.
She'd hold me tight and whisper, 'Soon your secret we will share.'
I could not help but say to her, 'Love, that will never be,'
For I never forgot those dying words my father said to me.

*'Keep your Dickey under your shirt my boy,' my father said to me,
'Keep it tightly covered, so no one else can see
The treasure you have hidden there, could fill your life with glee
Keep your Dickey under your shirt my boy,' my father said to me.*

We're married now for fourteen years with a big strong healthy son,
One day I'll ask the same of him as my old dad had done.
I hope he makes the promise when my secret I decree,
For I never forgot those dying words my father said to me

*'Keep your Dickey under your shirt my boy,' my father said to me,
'Keep it tightly covered, so no one else can see
The treasure you have hidden there, could fill your life with glee
Keep your Dickey under your shirt my boy,' my father said to me.*

*Keep your Dickey under your shirt - my - boy, my father -
said - to - me*

# INVENTIONS TO CATCH A DOG
## No 1 Kennel Scoop

# INVENTIONS TO CATCH A DOG
## No 2 Magnetic Lead

# INVENTIONS TO CATCH A DOG
## No 3 Hydraulic Dog Coat

# INVENTIONS TO CATCH A DOG
## No 4 Net Catcher

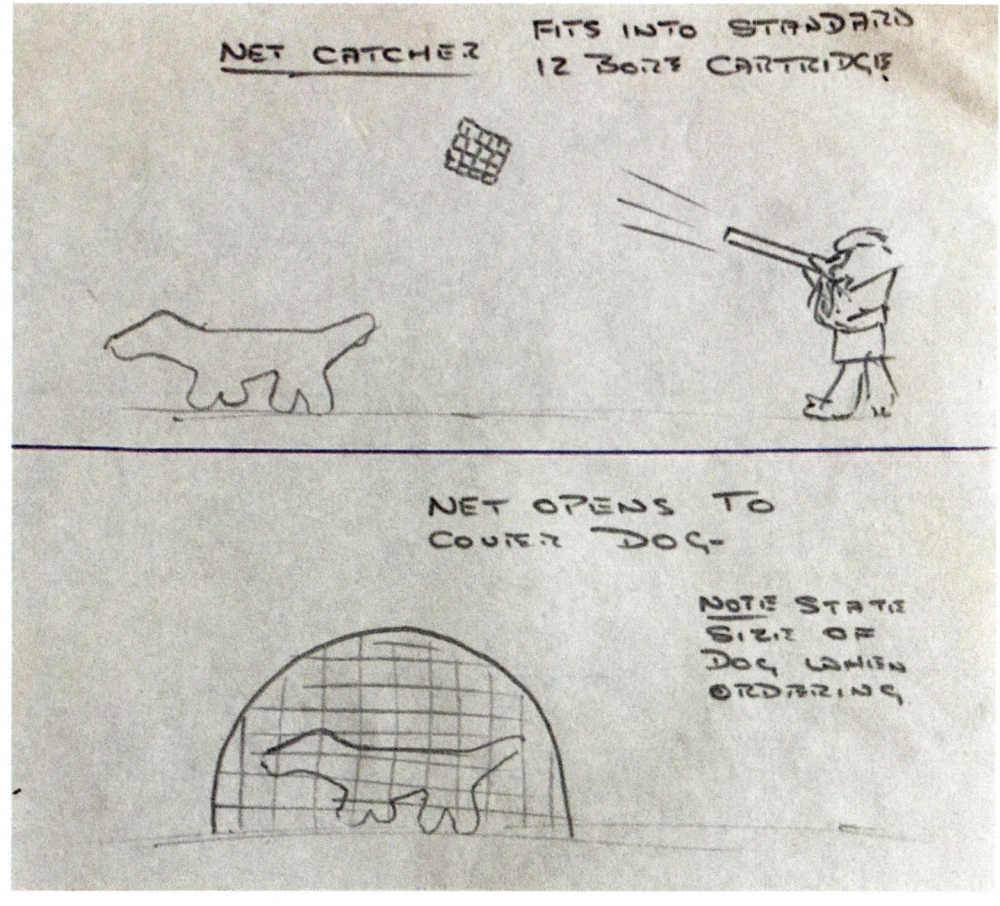

# INVENTIONS TO CATCH A DOG
## No 5 The Fatal Catcher

# CHRISTMAS COMES EARLY IN TED'S HOUSE

Ted was awoken by noise coming from the kitchen below. Crockery was breaking and he could hear his mother singing Christmas carols. Ted rushed into the kitchen just as his mother banged the oven door shut. 'At last,' she said, 'I have been trying to get that turkey in there for over half an hour.' Ted looked into the oven and saw a distressed turkey looking out through the glass door.

'But it's still alive, Mother,' said Ted.

'I wondered what was wrong,' she said, 'maybe that's why I had so much trouble stuffing it.' Ted opened the oven door and a perspiring, confused turkey jumped out and escaped through the open back door leaving a trail of steam behind it.

Ted's mum was complaining that they had not received one Christmas present or card this year. 'Maybe,' said Ted, 'Just maybe it's got something to do with it only being the 10$^{th}$ of September.'

'Yes,' she said, 'But last year I missed being at home at Christmas, I was in hospital after falling from the top of the Christmas tree. I told your father we should we should be like normal people and have a fairy or star on the top instead of me.' Ted's mum said she had decided not to put any money in the Christmas puddings this year as last year was a bit of a failure. Ted pointed out that it should be coins, not five pound notes.

Ted phoned the RSPCA as he was worried about the turkey and was assured it was ok, it had gone to an undisclosed address and given a new identity.

Ted sat down for breakfast with his mum and they talked about the year so far. It had started sadly with the death of his uncle Isaiah, given this name because he had a very religious father named Amos. His uncle's full name was Isaiah Chapter 1. He had three sons, Isaiah Chapter 2 and Isaiah Chapter 3. He named the third son George after he found out the gasman had been calling to read the meter three times a week over the previous two years.

Dear uncle Isaiah Chapter 1 committed suicide at his golf club by throwing himself onto his golf bag in front of his friends. They said at the inquest they had been trying to talk him down off the roof all morning, but he insisted he could not continue to live with a handicap. Ted's aunt was very angry and said he did it without giving any thought for her at all, where did he think she would be able to sell a bag of bent and broken golf clubs? She is coping very well with his death by again having the gas meter read three times a week, she said it seems to work better than counselling. Ted's mum thinks she made the right choice, she could not see how they could understand her problem as they usually only deal with council tax, wheelie-bins and planning applications.

Ted had another uncle called Spot, who was given this name by his father who really wanted a dog. The first things his father taught Spot were to sit, fetch a ball, and bark when the doorbell rang. He never got out of the habit of chasing the postman down the garden path. The down side of all this is he only had two baths a year. Uncle Spot was always claiming that one-day he would invent something that would change the world. Early in the year news came that he had at last invented something, but his next task was to decide what it was. He was a very quiet man and would sit in a chair for days in very deep thought. On two occasions his wife had called in the undertaker and on the last occasion, if his mobile phone had not gone off during the last hymn, he would have been buried.

The summer holiday was something different this year; it was the first time Ted and his mum and dad had been in an aeroplane. There was a little problem as they boarded the aircraft when Ted's mum demanded to sit beside the pilot. She claimed she could not ride in the back and must be able to see where she was going. They had been flying for a short time when Ted's mother said she had overheard someone talking about the Mile High Club and suggested to his dad that they should join it. Ted's dad said he had come on holiday to enjoy himself and he didn't want to talk about it.

The plane landed in Iceland and they transferred to their hotel for the night. Ted was getting excited as they were going whale-watching the very next day. Ted's mum said she had always wanted to go to Iceland as she had a favourite aunt who used to work on a whale-watching ship. She was big, weighing in at forty eight stones, so if no whales appeared they would lower her off the stern to swim around for the tourists. She sadly lost the job after she collided with an Icelandic fishing patrol ship.

Ted's great aunt stayed in the tourist business swimming around Loch Ness but lost this job after a complaint from Air Traffic Control who said she was coming up on radar and endangering the RAF low altitude pilot training. Air Traffic Control later gave her an identification number as they found she still came up on radar when going to the shops. Ted's mum recalled that this was a low time for her aunt so she came and stayed with them to help her recovery. While there, her aunt brought more to the house than anyone could imagine, bringing a lot of happiness to the family until the police came and took it all back. Ted's mum said tears came to her eyes as her aunt waved from the back of the police van.

The next day of their holiday they had boarded the ship and set off on the whale-watching trip. Ted had been a bit disappointed with his dad who said it was a waste of time because it was very misty and Wales was over seven hundred miles away, but Ted soon put him right saying it must be over a thousand. They had been sailing for over an hour and had not seen any sign of a whale and the other tourists were starting to complain to the captain who assured them he would solve the problem. The captain came over and suggested to Ted's mother that she should go below and look through a porthole. The captain said he was convinced that with her thin body and face like a harpoon she was making the whales nervous, and having a rope tied around her ankle to stop her falling overboard was not helping.

The journey back from holiday did not go without incident. Ted's dad went a bit silly and put his arm around Ted's mum as they came through customs. He was promptly arrested and held by customs for three hours on suspicion of trying to smuggle an ancient Egyptian mummy into the country. Ted's dad was released after an expert decided she was from a later period and was possibly from a totally different part of the world.

As Ted and his mum thought back over the year they could not help but remember that morning in July. As they all sat having breakfast the postman had arrived bringing a wedding invitation to them all from Ted's aunt, wife of deceased uncle Isaiah Chapter 1. She was planning to marry the gasman in August. They were all invited and she would like Ted's dad to give her away. Later that day, while Ted's mum had gone to the shops, he overheard his dad on the phone to the gasman, begging to give him Ted's mum instead. Ted was horrified at the thought of his dad giving his mum away, she must be worth something, he thought.

The wedding had been the highlight of the year so far; a grand affair, officiated over by local vicar, the Rev Wind. He was the same vicar who had performed the ceremony at Ted's parents' wedding. Ted's dad had not spoken to him since that day, claiming that all men should be breathalysed in the church before being married. The stores at the gas depot had loaned the groom a new boiler suit for the occasion. As a token of respect, Ted's aunt had decided to wear the pair of trousers that her late husband had been wearing on the fateful day he jumped from the golf club roof. She wore matching golfing shoes, jumper and cap, and she carried a golf bag with trailing nine iron. The bride was given away by Ted's dad after he had given the groom his last chance to change his mind and take up the offer he made over the phone in July. They left the church under an arch of burning gas blow-torches. Ted's aunt got slightly singed but was promptly covered in foam as a precaution.

The reception was held at the gas depot. Smoking was strictly forbidden, as there was a slight smell of gas in the room. Ted sat at a table with his mum, several other friends and relatives, and felt honoured to have the Rev Wind and his daughter Gail with them. Her father said she was a lovely, clever girl who looked at the weather forecast on television every night to see if she got a mention. Ted's mum's cousin Angus arrived from Aberdeen. His father bred Highland cattle. He was sorry to be a bit late but was pleased he could make the reception, and he sat down beside the vicar. He said hello to everyone he knew and then looked the vicar straight in the eyes and in his broad Scottish accent said, 'Arre yous parson wind?'

Ted's mum was horrified. 'Angus,' she said, 'How could you suggest such a thing, the reverend wouldn't do that in company.' Ted's cousins, Isaiah Chapter 2, Isaiah Chapter 3 and George, said a few words. The gasman's eldest son said a few words on behalf of his other twenty-seven brothers and sisters. The bride and groom left in the works van for a week's honeymoon in a two star hotel overlooking the Bacton Gas Terminal in Norfolk.

As Ted and his mum finished breakfast she said, "Ted it was lovely thinking back through the year, let's get this Christmas over and hope next year will be just as good".

## SEA LEVELS
*Composed October 2010*

They say the sea is rising
They say it's down to us
They say we should all be concerned
But what is all the fuss?

They say the caps are melting
And bringing up the sea
They say it's global warming
This makes no sense to me.

They say the ice fills up the sea
With nowhere else to go,
But then the ice floats higher
It's the same old "status quo".

Is it the ban on whaling
That makes the waters rise?
A lot of water is dispersed
For the whale is of great size.

Governments won't let it go
The tax is worth a lot
Science should apply more logic
I think they've lost the plot.

So let us use some common sense
And think about the rain
It's pumped along into our taps
Then we pour it down the drain

The drains run to the rivers
It's the place for them to go
Water from the mountains
Make the rivers overflow.

Why has science never noticed?
For it's very plain to me
Rivers all around the world
Run downhill to the sea.

It's been going on since time began
How come they didn't know?
The seas will just keep filling up
And one day, will overflow.

# MY COUSIN SID
*Composed December 2013*

Some say the world did not evolve
Others say it did
So, to settle this for once and all
I asked my cousin Sid.

Sid says there was no big bang
For that was never right
If the world had started with a bang
It would have woke me up last night.

Sid's got the know and how of it
He's got two GCEs
One for digging spuds up
And one for shelling peas.

Sid went to his school reunion
To the teacher his mother wrote
'Sorry for Sid's thirty year absence
Please accept this apology note.'

Sid met many friends from school days
Now bankers in Mercs and such
When asked what he did for a living
Sid said, 'I try not to do very much.'

Sid one day hopes to marry
He's already got the ring
His problem now is finding a girl
With a finger to fit the thing.

Sid had a problem sleeping
'Count sheep,' some people said
Sid says, 'It didn't work for me
I'd rather be in bed.'

If you should ever meet him
You'll sure be pleased you did
For you'll find no better guy on earth
Than my dear cousin Sid.

# DRESSING UP DOGS
*Wardrobe by John Mason*

TIGER THE LURCHER

MEGANS FALSE TEETH!

# FORGET THE PAST
*Composed December 2018*

Alone in the dark, simply drifting
Level days, nothing uplifting
The darkness screened, your presence near
No one in my life, no one to care

Our parallel lives so near, yet far
Later shone on, by a passing star
It saw us missing the occasional touch
It knew we could love and enjoy so much

And when the star, it got it right
Putting light on that long dark night
It chose a moment, just for some
Parallel lives, were joined as one

Enjoying the moments we spend together
Working hard to keep the tether
The spaces filled with careful measure
Which we both love, need and treasure

I am glad we found that inner you
The part you thought did not shine through
I saw you as you really are
And so did that bright, passing star

Leave past regrets without a trace
Live and enjoy that surprise embrace
Our world joined by that star above
We were made to meet, to hold and to love.

# THE WIGHTON PARROT

Dear Reader

The author cannot guarantee that what you are about to read is all fact. He may have added, using his great knowledge and imagination, events which in his opinion would, without any doubt, have taken place. Names, stories or locations may contain some embellishment.

The following story unravels 100 years of mystery, and sometimes fear, which clouded two Norfolk villages concerning an event which had taken place at the very end of the 19th century. On Wednesday 13th October 1897 the anger between these two villages boiled over and they found themselves locked in battle.

Many unsubstantiated stories, tales and pub yarns have been bandied about throughout the years which sparked the attention of the author. He had heard first hand, through his family, that there had been a battle but now could confirm that a battle had taken place, as he had checked and found there was a Wednesday in 1897.

It was known as 'The Battle of the Wighton Parrot'.

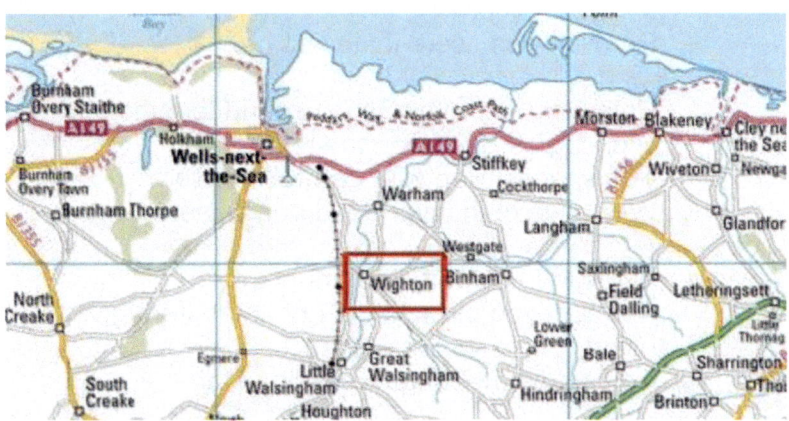

Records show that a few years before the battle, a very unusual parrot had been seen in various parts of the village of Wighton. It was always around in the evenings and spent the nights in the church tower. It was quite old when it arrived and it saddened the villagers of Wighton when it died after only a short stay. The dead parrot was taken to the Wighton pottery workshop where a young apprentice, who was a keen ornithologist, was pleased to take a close look at it. He decided there was nothing like it in any books he had, and thought it should be seen by someone more knowledgeable than himself.

Experts planned to come from far and wide but travel was very slow in the 1890s. The young apprentice was asked to make an exact copy of the parrot in clay before it deteriorated, which he did, and completed it in two weeks. During the work he had noticed that the parrot's left foot was exactly the same as its right foot, which struck him as very unusual. The apprentice then lovingly buried the remains of the parrot somewhere outside the village. In the next few months, experts filed through the workshop and a final meeting to discuss their findings was held in the church rooms.

After much deliberation, they decided the bird had close similarities with a Steppe Eagle so had flown, or been blown by strong winds, to Wighton from the Himalayas. They believed it was the only one in existence at the time, and was now extinct. It was pointed out by the experts that you needed to look very closely at the two right feet as that was the only feature that makes it a unique parrot.

After they left, the young apprentice, not knowing what to do with his creation, decided, to make it into a lamp to light the church room, to the delight of the Wighton vicar. The vicar of the adjoining village of Hindringham heard of the lamp's existence and, the following Sunday, decided to tell his parishioners that as the parrot had spent all day feeding in their village, they should claim the lamp as theirs to light their own church room. He duly approached the vicar of Wighton and claimed ownership of the parrot lamp. His claim was rejected by the vicar, so the Hindringham vicar said, 'Then we have no option but to fight you for it.'

Old Sneezer, a Wighton smallholder, offered his meadow for the battle, on the understanding that they did not dig any trenches or frighten his pigs, and they would clear up afterwards. The battle was due to be fought on Tuesday, but it rained, so was put off until the next day.

Wednesday came and fighting men from both villages assembled, armed with the only permitted battle weapons: forks, spades, hoes or rakes. Old Sneezer thought he would have a go, but decided to fight for the Hindringham side to even up the numbers. The parrot lamp was placed on a milking stool, mid-way between the two sides, and closely guarded by the two vicars. The vicars had been told to get the battle going without delay, as the cowman wanted the milking stool back in the parlour by 4 o'clock for afternoon milking.

As is so often the case, both vicars suddenly decided that they needed a new roof on the church, so agreed to take a collection before the battle could begin, as there might be fewer people to donate after it. They were quite pleased with the collection which included two slates off one of Old Sneezer's pig sties. They conducted a short blessing and declared the battle should commence by ringing a hand bell and shouting, 'Go for it boys, and knock the hell out of each other.'

Within seconds the fighting was raging and casualties began to appear, as already the blacksmith had lost the false teeth he had made the day before, two pairs of trousers had come off, and old Alf lost his wedding ring so never went back home to his wife. It was recorded that old Stinker Long took off his trousers and used them as a weapon, causing havoc to both sides. It was rumoured they had not been completely off since his 16$^{th}$ birthday. (Here the author advises caution, he was not happy to include that last statement, as it did not make clear the age of Stinker Long at the time).

One of the Hindringham men went home and told his wife the Wighton men were not fighting fairly, so she came and had a word with the leader of the Wighton men. Because of the noise they went behind the pig sty to discuss it, and she left the battlefield holding his hand and never returned home.

The vicars decided that, as the battle was now gathering a nice steady momentum and should last most of the day, they would move to the quietness of the Wighton pub and record all the people taking part in the battle. The Wighton vicar didn't have a pencil, and the Hindringham vicar didn't trust him so refused to lend him his, but he did buy the beer.

The battle went on for twenty minutes. It would have gone on longer but suddenly the Wighton fighters called a halt. They announced it was 1 o'clock and they had brought a packed lunch, and fighting could resume after. During the break, all the fighters were shocked to see that the vicars had departed and the milking stool was still there, but the parrot lamp had gone. Both sides agreed that there was no point in continuing with the battle, and decided to retire to the pub. They found the two vicars at the pub who swore on the Bible that neither of them had stolen the parrot lamp but, next Sunday they would pray for its safe return. Needless to say, that didn't work, and the parrot lamp remained missing for many years.

A memorial to the battle, in the form of an upturned toilet bucket, surrounded with Wighton flints, was erected on the green at the top of Wighton Hill. As no names were recorded it was just inscribed with the date 1897.

The story now moves on 43 years to 1940, when the author was 6 years old. He arrived with his mother from London, to stay with his grandmother in a farm cottage just outside the village of Wighton. He was thrilled to find that he had a great uncle George who had fought and been wounded in The Battle of the Wighton Parrot. The author would sit and listen for hours as his great uncle relived the details of the battle, and told of an injury he received which resulted in a hernia and the need to wear a leather truss for the rest of his life.

One day, the author and his mother went for an overnight stay with a favourite aunt and, on returning the next day to grandmother's house, were met with devastating news. Grandmother told them that dear great uncle George was dead. He had died at 97 as a direct result of the injury he received in the Wighton battle, and she felt a compensation claim should be made. She went on to say how he had been out for a few pints, got up in the night and tripped over his leather truss, which he had left on the landing, causing him to fall down the stairs breaking his neck and dying from his injuries. She went on to say, 'It's so sad, if he had not had to wear that leather truss he would not have suffered such a premature death and would still be with us.'

The upturned toilet bucket memorial of the battle on the village green was now nothing more than a small rusty mark, surrounded by Wighton flints. Grandmother decided that she was sure great uncle George would have wanted the leather truss to rest there to mark his part in the Wighton battle. The local harness maker carefully stitched a lovely '*GEORGE*' onto it and on the day of his funeral the family gathered and said a few words, as grandmother gently placed the leather truss on the rust spot in the middle of the stone circle. The truss was stolen a few weeks later, it is thought by the harness maker, as he never got paid for his work.

The story now moves to a more serious level. A few weeks later the author moved with his mother to a small cottage in Wighton, where she had acquired a job as a live in housekeeper for a man called Dod and his son Henry. The first thing the author's mother did was to cook a lovely meal. Dod apologised for the wobbly table but explained, he had made it using four second hand artificial wooden legs, and the people were of different heights, but he liked the shape and feet. Henry cleared the table and washed up. The author was left thinking, 'How can you have 'second hand legs?', but children did not ask questions in those days.

With no electricity in the village at that time, when darkness came, Henry fetched and stood a fascinating lamp on the table. The author being only 6 years old asked 'what sort of light is that?' Henry, giving the glass a final polish said 'It's a parrot lamp'. The author looked in awe at the lamp and was saying over and over in his little mind Henry's magic words, 'It's a parrot lamp, it's a parrot lamp, it's parrot lamp'. The author has never forgotten those words, and they are still as fresh in his mind now, as they were the day they were first spoken to him. At that time neither the author, nor his mother, knew the parrot lamp was connected with the battle that great uncle George had fought in. The author went to bed still pondering second hand legs but, hoped most of all to dream about the parrot lamp. He could not wait to see it again tomorrow.

After living in the cottage for about two years, Henry got a job about 15 miles away and the author and his mother moved with him, leaving Dod alone in the cottage. An older brother of the author also came to live with them in the new home.

A few years later, with the Wighton battle now long forgotten, the author was passing through the village when he stopped at the local pub. New toilets had been installed and builders were starting to demolish the old urinal. The old whitewash had peeled off the walls and exposed some names. On closer examination it was revealed that 60 years ago the Wighton vicar, (not having a pencil) had scratched on the wall all the names of the Wighton men involved in the The Battle of the Wighton Parrot. However, the author was disturbed to find that, despite checking the whole wall several times, he could see no mention of his great uncle George on the list. He went into the bar, got a drink and tried to unravel in his mind what he had seen. He had heard the stories first hand from the man he admired, great uncle George himself. It must be a terrible mistake. The author tried to think of his next move.

Suddenly the penny dropped. 'I'm in Wighton,' he thought, 'Why not go to the house where I saw the parrot lamp as a boy in 1940? It's a long shot but, is Dod still living there?'

It was a short walk to the house. The author knocked on the door. It was a little time before the door opened and there was Dod. After some explanation he remembered the author and invited him in. Nothing had changed in the house and Dod was now in his nineties. Knowing that the parrot lamp had gone missing during the battle, and assuming he still had it, the author told Dod that a list of names had been found on an old wall at the pub and said how disappointed he was at not finding his great uncle George named as having fought in the battle, as he had told the family so much about it. Dod went very quiet, and decided to make a cup of tea.

They sat drinking the tea and, after a while Dod said, 'You may not like what I am about to tell you lad, but you may as well hear it. It is true that your great uncle George was wounded during the The Battle of the Wighton Parrot, but he was not actually in the battle. He was watching it through an opening in the hedge. After watching the battle for some time he noticed the two vicars walk out of the meadow, leaving the parrot lamp unguarded. Seizing the opportunity, he went through the opening and grabbed the parrot lamp off the milking stool. As he turned to leave, a short-sighted Wighton fighter, seeing something move, hurled a large Wighton flint at it. The flint struck the parrot lamp, knocking out an eye, chipping its beak and knocking off its left foot. The missile continued on and struck great uncle George in his lower abdomen.

'With the parrot lamp under his arm, and extreme pain running down his left leg, he limped towards the village.' Dod was standing at his front gate when he saw great uncle George coming towards him. George had told him the whole story and asked for help as he must not be seen stealing the parrot lamp.

Dod now told the author how, three days before, he had himself suffered a similar pain. As luck had it, a travelling salesman/doctor visited the village once a month giving advice and selling medicines, artificial wooden legs, in fact, anything he could get away with, and this was his day. He took one look at Dod, diagnosed a hernia and sold him a leather truss for 3 pence in old money. He then drove off at great speed in his pony and trap. Dod went indoors, dropped his trousers, and his Sunday pipe complete with tobacco fell out from behind his belt - so much for a hernia! He now had a leather truss surplus to requirements. Dod, feeling a little bit cheated, got comfort from the fact that he had had a good deal with him in the recent past. He was doing a special offer of four artificial wooden legs for the price of two. Dod said 'I took him up on it and made this table.'

Dod assured great uncle George he could help him. 'That Wighton flint hitting your abdomen has given you a hernia and you will need a leather truss.'

'It's another four weeks before the travelling salesman/doctor comes,' said great uncle George, 'Where am I going to get one of those?'

'Well,' Dod replied, 'Knowing how quickly hernias can happen, I always keep one handy and, as a friend, I will let you have it for 5 pence in old money.'

'I've only got 4 pence in old money,' said great uncle George, sadly.

'Not a problem' said Dod, 'Give me the 4 pence in old money plus the lamp and the leather truss is yours'.

'DONE!' bellowed great uncle George.

'You have been,' said Dod, handing over the leather truss. Dropping his trousers, great uncle George fitted the leather truss without delay. Dod watched great uncle George go off towards home, now walking much more evenly, as he was hopping on both legs instead of only one.

Having known and trusted great uncle George, and later spoken with Dod, the author was left with the thinking that he shouldn't believe anything he hears, sees or touches, but hold it in abeyance until he has confirmed it for himself.

On the 100 year anniversary of this event, and due to a very important find, the author decided to try to solve the long standing mystery of the parrot lamp, resulting in the above story, which he hopes you have found both interesting and enlightening.

He had been moved out of the family home since the 1960s. In 1997 with both his mother and Henry no longer with us, his older brother asked if there was anything in the back bedroom he wanted before it went into the council rubbish bin. To his delight the author found, covered in dust and cobwebs, the parrot lamp complete with the glass unbroken. It had been brought there when Henry had cleared his father Dod's house at Wighton several years before.

The author did consider giving the parrot lamp back to the Wighton people but it may have resulted in another falling out between the villages. He chose instead to commit all his findings to paper for future reference. The parrot lamp remained, deteriorating, in his garden shed for over 20 years.

One day, a lady, who was now spending a lot of time at his house, came out of the shed carrying the parrot lamp. 'What's this?' she asked.

'That's the parrot lamp,' the author replied. He then had to explain, as he has done many times since, what made it a parrot lamp.

'Why is it in such a sad state?' the lady asked. 'It's worth restoring and I can do it!'

In 2018 the parrot lamp was fully restored, layers of old paint were removed from the base. It was given a new eye and left foot, the beak repaired and the whole parrot cleaned.

It now resides at a secret location, somewhere in Norfolk.

*The newly restored parrot lamp*

## COVID 19
*A lockdown poem*

Mexico's Corona beer is not selling
The virus has made sure of that
They feel the whole world needs telling
The stuff's piling up in the vat.

For the people who went shopping early
And left all the shelves looking bare
You should now feel guilt and then surely
Come forward to help out with the beer.

Six pints a night for the rest of the year
Is not much to ask of a hog
The toilet rolls that you selfishly bought
Will help with your time on the bog.


## LIFES TOO SHORT

Its sometimes just forgiving
If the sentence is too long
If Janets pen just makes a slip
And spels the words al rong.

Does it matter if Toms jackets tight
Fabric stretching under strain
Toms brain will still be happy
As it still keeps out the rain.

Itll be sorted in the end
If Jacks car just will not start
Bills garage van is full of spares
Hes sure to have the part.

So why be sad with the omission
For surely you can see
It still makes sense when reading
Without the apostrophe.

## THE LAST PORK PIE
*Composed in 2021*

Big Ballroom Barry donned his mask,
And walked into the store
The last remaining pie was left
There won't be any more.

Big Barry was the last in line,
In front were only two,
They didn't look, like pork pie eaters,
But then, people never do.

Big Barry, keeping two metres clear,
Could not hear what was said,
But the man looked at the lone pork pie,
And bought two sausage rolls instead.

One lady customer, in front of him,
His tension running high,
This lady looked up market, yes,
The smoked salmon type, walked by.

The pie was now a metre forth,
When he had to stop, right dead,
Waltzing Walter, in contraflow,
Was unmasked, two metres ahead.

Walter looked at the pie, in earnest,
It was truly in his sights,
Big Barry threw a warning,
'Touch that pie and I'll put out your lights'.

Other customers, at social distance,
Not surprised at the sound in their ears,
For the dancing rivalry, in the Village Hall,
Has been going on for years.

But this time it was different,
With a principle involved,
If Walter used the one way scheme,
The problem could be solved.

A 'social distance' crowd, had gathered,
For the likes they'd never seen,
Two men in anger, two metres apart,
And a pork pie in between.

Old Godfrey walked towards the pair
'With a mask Walter would comply,
'I'll put my pants upon your head,
And hope you do not die.'

The crowd knew Big Barry was dangerous,
And Walter should give him some ground,
His quickstep with fishtail included,
Was not only good, but renowned.

The Police arrived, armed at the ready,
The inspector looked at the two,
'They're masked, distanced and complying,
I don't see there's much I can do'.

DJ Jock, was in there shopping,
With Loose Lily, standing near,
'Distraction is the plan in mind,
You'll have to grab my gear',

Loose Lily moved without delay,
Two metres was no bar,
'Stop!' said Jock, 'I don't mean that,
Get it from my car'.

The DJ reached out for a record,
And played one straight from stock,
The two hard men started waltzing,
But the DJ was playing Punk Rock.

Martha Smith, would have her moment,
Through the chink in her front door,
The TV crew were streaming live,
As they had done, many times before.

'I saw Police, and flashing lights a going,
I asked Hubby, what that was all about,
Ya dun't expect that ta happen here,
I can tell ya, I wun't be going out'.

At the shop the standoff was ever tense,
And closing time drew nigh,
When a shop girl shouted, 'we're closing down',
And walked off with the pie.

'We've been here, all day, you can't do that',
Big Barry, was heard to shout,
'It's too late now,' the girl replied,
'The sell-by date's run out.'

*Covid restrictions were observed during the writing of this poem.*

## NOT JUST A DOG

*Composed July 2022, in memory of a beautiful rescue dog*

Saved from a sad, uncertain start
As people saunter by
My problem now is catch a heart
As I look them in the eye.

I hope someone will like me
And put me to the test
I'll give them love, and let them see
Me do my very best.

Two people said they'd take me
Now I have a lovely home
They also have a dog you see
So I won't be on my own.

They named me Merlot, after a wine
But I have no grumbles at all
A name I think will suit me just fine
When I hear it, I'll come back first call.

My sport is, let's run a hare, or a rabbit
With my friend we do it quite well
My owners think it a bad habit
But it's natural for us you can tell

The unfailing love you have given me
To my family, I hope I gave pleasure
As I ran on the beach, and sniffed the cool sea
Can I leave you these memories to treasure?

          Love xxx